Dear Parent:
Your child's love o̶_____ ̶ere!

Every child learns to read in _____ ̶er own speed.
You can help your young reade̶._____ ̶e confident
by encouraging his or her own interests and abilities. ̶o̶o̶ can also guide
your child's spiritual development by reading stories with biblical values
and Bible stories, like I Can Read! books published by Zonderkidz. From
books your child reads with you to the first books he or she reads alone,
there are I Can Read! books for every stage of reading:

SHARED READING
Basic language, word repetition, and whimsical
illustrations, ideal for sharing with your emergent reader.

BEGINNING READING
Short sentences, familiar words, and simple concepts for
children eager to read on their own.

READING WITH HELP
Engaging stories, longer sentences, and language play
for developing readers.

READING ALONE
Complex plots, challenging vocabulary, and high-interest
topics for the independent reader.

ADVANCED READING
Short paragraphs, chapters, and exciting themes for the
perfect bridge to chapter books.

I Can Read! books have introduced children to the joy of reading since
1957. Featuring award-winning authors and illustrators and a fabulous
cast of beloved characters, I Can Read! books set the standard for
beginning readers.

A lifetime of discovery begins with the magical words **"I Can Read!"**

Visit www.icanread.com for information on enriching your child's reading experience.
Visit www.zonderkidz.com for more Zonderkidz I Can Read! titles.

"Speak the truth to each other."
Zechariah 8:16

ZONDERKIDZ

Junior Comes Clean
©2013 Big Idea Entertainment, LLC. VEGGIETALES®, character names, likenesses
and other indicia are trademarks of and copyrighted by Big Idea Entertainment, LLC.
All rights reserved.
Illustrations ©2011 by Big Idea Entertainment, Inc.

Requests for information should be addressed to:
Zonderkidz, 5300 Patterson SE, Grand Rapids, Michigan 49530

ISBN: 978-0-310-73208-2

Editor: Mary Hassinger
Art direction: Karen Poth
Cover design: Karen Poth
Interior design: Ron Eddy

Printed in China

13 14 15 16 17 18 /DSC/ 20 19 18 17 16 15 14 13 12 11 10 9 8 7 6 5 4 3 2

I Can Read!

Junior Comes Clean

story by Karen Poth

My name is Detective Larry.

This is my partner, Bob.

We solve mysteries.

Sometimes our jobs

are very messy.

Here is one of our stories.

Bob and I were in the car.

RING!

A call came in.

It was Mom Asparagus.

I drove there—FAST!

Junior's room was a mess.

A BIG mess.

Junior sat in the corner.

He looked scared.

"What happened?" Bob asked.

"I didn't do it," Junior said.

9

"Bad guys did this," Junior said.

"I couldn't stop them."

"That sounds awful," I said.

"That sounds strange," Bob said.

11

We left Junior's house.

While we were in the car,

another call came in.

It was Junior's mom again.

We drove back to
Junior's house.
This mess was worse.
Milk was spilled all over.

I drew a chalk outline
around the spill.

"Tell us what happened," Bob said.

"I heard a crash,"
Mom said.
"I found Junior here
with this mess."

"I didn't do it!" Junior said.

"It was the bad guys!

They spilled the milk and ran."

I checked
for fingerprints.
"What did the
bad guys look like?"
I asked.

"There were three bad guys,"
Junior said.

"A zucchini and two brussels sprouts."

"Brussels sprouts," I said.

"We should have known."

"There is more," said Junior's dad.

"Come with me."

We went upstairs.

Junior's room was clean!

But there was a pile

under the rug.

I tripped on it.

Bob lifted the rug.
All of Junior's toys
were piled under it.

"The bad guys did it,"
Junior said.
"I tried to stop them."

"You tried to stop them?" Bob asked.

Junior looked scared again.

"Junior, are you sure
you are telling the truth?" Bob asked.
Junior was quiet.

Junior sat on the bed.

His dad sat next to him.

"Is there something
you would like to say?"
Dad asked.

"Telling lies is never
a good thing to do."

"I did it," Junior said.

"I made the mess.

I spilled the milk.

And I hid everything under my rug,"

Junior said.

"I'm sorry."

"I'm glad you told the truth," Dad said. "God wants us to tell the truth."

Junior smiled.

"Will you forgive me?" he asked.

"Of course, we forgive you,"
Mom said.

"Now, go and clean up."

We left the
Asparagus house.
Everyone was smiling!
Case closed.